Contents

A Note from the Author

This book started because of a boy I knew called Nick. His dad was a racing driver, and he drove very fast on the road. He was killed when his car hit a tree. Nick grew up to be a racing driver too, and he's OK.

My story is about a girl, because some girls like speed just as much as boys do. I still like to drive fast – but only on wide roads when there is no-one else about.

To anyone who likes going fast.
Be careful!

Published in 2006 in Great Britain by
Barrington Stoke Ltd
www.barringtonstoke.co.uk

ISBN-10: 1-84299-413-1
ISBN-13: 978-1-84299-413-9

Printed in Great Britain by Bell & Bain Ltd

Chapter 1
Deb

My dad died in a car crash. His car skidded and he hit a tree. He wasn't driving badly. He was a great driver. He was a good mechanic, too. He ran the garage where Mum and I still live.

My dad showed me how to drive when I was ten, on the car park behind the garage. I'm 16 now. I can't wait to drive on the road.

Ted lets me drive cars in and out of the garage, but he says, "Deb, do be careful." Ted is my mum's new man. He runs the garage now. He's good with cars but he's not like my dad. No one is like my dad. Ted tries to be nice, but he's boring.

School is boring, too. I work in the garage on Saturdays, and Ted pays me. I sell petrol and put air in tyres and check oil. I wish I could work on cars. I wish I could be a mechanic like Dad, but mechanics have to pass exams and go to College. I hate exams. So I'll go on selling petrol.

****

Mick Dobb came in for petrol yesterday. He rides this massive bike, a Honda. I love bikes.

I filled the tank for him. I said, "I watch the bike racing on TV. That guy Rossi is great, he wins all the time."

Mick said, "I don't like Rossi. He's not riding with Hondas any more. Dirty rat. Hondas are best."

I said, "I've always wanted a go on a big bike."

"Great," said Mick. "No problem. I'll pick you up tomorrow night. 7.30, OK?"

I can't wait.

****

It was brilliant with Mick on the bike. What a buzz! The wind in my face, the roar of the engine, the speed – I felt super-alive. We went past the cars so fast, they looked like they were standing still.

Mick shouted over his shoulder, "We're doing a ton! That's 100 m.p.h."

I yelled, "WOW! YES!"

There's a café where all the bikers go
and we stopped there for a drink.

All the bikers' girls have dead smart
gear. Mick had lent me a leather jacket and
a crash helmet, but they were a bit big. I
need to get some gear of my own, but it
costs a bomb. I'll save up the money Ted
gives me for selling petrol.

Mum was waiting for me when I got in.

"What time do you call this?" she said.
"I've been worried sick. Look, Deb, I don't

want you hanging about with bikers. Bikes are dangerous. And that boy Mick is nuts. My friend Joy says he's been done for speeding twice, and he's only 19."

I said, "Your friend Joy is a silly old cow."

Mum blew up, of course, and we had a flaming row. I don't care. I like Mick. He got two teeth knocked out in a crash last year, but he's dead sexy. I'm going out with him again tonight.

Chapter 2
Bikes

This morning Ted said, "Deb, I'll get you a car when you're 17. Birthday present."

"Go on?" I said. "What sort?"

"Not a new one. I don't have that much money. I'll get a good old one and show you how to do it up. You'll get to know a lot about cars that way."

I said, "Thanks."

I think it was Mum's idea. She hates Mick, and she hates bikes. I bet she asked Ted to get me a car so I'd stop thinking about bikes.

I don't see why Mum hates bikes. My dad didn't die in a bike crash. He was driving a car. I dream about it sometimes.

Wet road, car skidding. Hit the tree. It's a bad dream.

"Mum," I said, "why do you have this thing about bikes? Cars can be dangerous, too."

She said, "Cars aren't dangerous. It's the way people drive them."

I said, "It's the same with bikes. They're not dangerous with a good rider."

"Bikes have only got two wheels," Mum said. "That's dangerous. And Mick Dobb is not a good rider."

"Yes, he is," I said. He's fantastic."

"He's been done for speeding twice," Mum said. "And he got smashed up in a crash. That's not fantastic, it's stupid."

I can't talk to her when she's like that. So I walked off.

****

I got my own crash helmet today. Mick took me to a shop where the stuff is cheap. He checked that the helmet fitted right, but I paid for it. I'll get a jacket when I've saved up some more money.

We went for a burn down the motorway after that. My new crash helmet is great, it makes me feel like a real biker.

Mick says there's a party on Saturday. All his biker mates are going to it. I know a lot of them now, and their girlfriends, too. It's at Sally's house. I like Sally. She's

Don's girl friend, and he's one of Mick's mates.

I'm going to buy a new top. I've seen the one I want. It's red, with silver stars. I can only just afford it after buying the helmet. I want bike boots, too, but they cost a lot.

Mick's going to pick me up at eight, on the bike. The party's going to be brilliant, I can't wait.

Chapter 3
Party

Saturday night, I was all ready to go out. I'd washed my hair and done my make-up. I was wearing my new top. I had nothing to do but wait for Mick. The clock said eight but he didn't come. I waited and waited. He still didn't come. The clock said nine.

I rang his mobile.

"Oh, hi," he said.

"Mick – where are you?"

"I'm at this party. I got a lift with a
mate."

He sounded drunk. Or stoned, maybe.

I said, "Oh, great. What about me? You
said you'd pick me up."

"Yeah, well, sorry. Can't ride if I'm pissed, can I?"

I was mad. I said, "So how do I get there?"

"Get a lift with a mate?" he said. "Or drive. Yeah, that's it. You can drive a car, can't you?"

I heard a girl say, "Stop talking to her, you're with me."

Mick said to her, "Pack it in. No, no, stop it." She was trying to grab his phone, I think. Or something. Both of them were giggling.

I switched off.

Mum and Ted were out, so I couldn't get a lift. I wouldn't ask them, anyway.

I had to get to that party, to tell Mick Dobb he was a rat.

So I had to drive, didn't I?

The keys to all the cars were on hooks by the door. I'd take Ted's Mini. He lent it out to customers when he was working on their cars, so it was there for anyone to use. I'd driven it before, but only to park it.

Dad used to say, "If you can park a car, you can drive it anywhere."

Dad knew about things like that. He was a good driver.

The Mini was in the corner by the wall, behind the breakdown truck. If Mum and

Ted came back before I did, they'd never see it had gone. But I'd be quick. I'd just tell Mick what I thought of him then come back. I got in the car and started it up. I checked it had enough petrol. Yes, it was half full.

I backed the car out and turned it round. Then I started along the road.

I was very careful. I didn't speed. I went along the lane, not through the town. There are more police in the town. I didn't want them to see me. They don't like under-age drivers with no tax or insurance.

I didn't like it much, either, but I had to get to the party. Nothing would stop me.

****

I could hear the party when I got near the house, the music was so loud. I parked the car and locked it. Then I went to the house and banged on the door.

Sally opened it.

"Hi, Deb," she said. "You made it. Great."

The place was full of people. Sally gave me a can of cider.

"Thanks," I said. "Have you seen Mick?"

"He's over there," she said. Then she put her hand on my arm. "Deb, don't talk to him right now. He's kind of – with someone."

"Oh, yes?" I said. "Well, too bad."

I found Mick on a sofa with a girl in his lap.

"Having fun, are you?" I said.

"Oh, hi," said Mick. "You got here, then." He was grinning.

"Yes," I said. "I did."

I kicked his shins and poured my can of cider over him.

The girl got most of it. She jumped up
and tried to hit me, but her mates grabbed
her.

"Oh, shit," said Mick. "You cow." He
said a lot more, but I walked off. I'd done
what I wanted to. Now I was going home.

A boy said, "Deb, don't go. Let me get
you another can of cider."

He's called Alan. We went out in the
garden and sat under a tree.

It was still light. We talked a lot. Alan drives an ice cream van to make some money, but he's into cars and bikes like me. And he wants to be a mechanic.

"I hate exams, same as you," he said. "I messed it up at school, but I want to have another go. I'm starting evening classes in September. Why don't you come, too?"

I said, "Are you kidding? I'm too thick."

Alan said, "You're not thick. You're dead smart. It's just you never felt like work at school. Never saw it was important. You were bored, right?"

"Right," I said.

We both laughed. And he kissed me.

We went in when it started to get dark. Everyone was dancing. Mick was still on the sofa, flat out. The girl had gone. I

danced with Alan. I had some more cider but not a lot, because I had to drive the car.

It got late, and Alan said, "How are you getting home? I'll run you back on the bike if you like."

I said, "Thanks a lot, but I have to take the car home."

"You're driving?" Alan said. He looked a bit worried. We both knew why.

"Don't tell anyone," I said.

Alan said, "OK, I won't. But take care."

"Sure," I said.

I wished I could go with him on the bike.

Chapter 4
Disaster

The car's lights lit up the lane. A rabbit ran across in front of me. I braked, and it went into the hedge safely. That was good. I started to feel better about driving the car. I thought, *I'm a good driver, same as Dad.* I started to go faster.

It had been raining, and the car was splashing through mud and water, like rally driving. I'd love to do rally driving. I watch it on TV, cars going through rivers and up steep hills.

Sharp bend!

I'd been thinking about TV and rally driving. I was going too fast.

I hit the brakes.

The car skidded on the mud. It ran up the bank. I was thrown to one side, my arm hit the door. I pulled the wheel round. The car went on sliding, there was a big tree –

CRASH!

I was dreaming. The same dream I'd had so often, only this time it was me in this dream, not Dad.

It wasn't a dream. It was real.

My neck hurt. There was soft stuff all round me. I felt like I couldn't breathe.

The soft stuff was the air bags. They filled the space in front of me.

There was no sound. The engine had stopped.

I could smell petrol. I was scared the car might go on fire. The air bag was in my way and I couldn't reach the key to turn the

engine off. The driver's door was hanging open, so I squeezed out, then put my hand in and turned the key.

The car's lights went out. The lane was very dark.

My neck hurt a lot where the seat belt had cut in, but I was OK. I was alive.

I heard my dad's voice in my ear.

You were lucky, he said. *You got away with it. I didn't.*

A cloud of steam was coming up from the engine. I could just see it in the dark. The front of the car was a total mess. No hope of driving it home.

I wished I was with Alan, on his bike. But I was here, on my own.

There was only one thing to do, and it was going to be awful.

I dug in the back of the crashed car for my bag and got out my mobile.

I had to phone home.

Chapter 5
Ted

"You idiot," yelled Mum. "You total prat!"

"Mum, please – "

"What do you mean, 'Mum, please'? What did you *think* I'd say?"

I was crying. "I know. I'm sorry."

Then she was sorry, too. She said, "Darling, are you all right? Are you hurt?"

"I'm OK," I sobbed, "but I don't know what to do."

"Hang on."

I heard her calling Ted. I didn't want to hear what she was telling him. Then he picked up the phone.

"Where are you, love?" he asked. He sounded calm, as always. "I'll come and get you."

It seemed a long wait, alone in the dark. I got very cold. I didn't have a jacket. I started to shiver. At last I saw car lights coming.

Ted was in the breakdown truck. He got out and looked at the Mini.

"Well," he said, "you made quite a job of that."

I was crying again. "I'm sorry," I said. "I'm really sorry."

"Come on," he said. "Let's get you in the truck. It's warm in there."

He helped me get in and put a blanket round me. He'd got a flask of tea and he gave me some. Then he went back to the car. He left the truck's lights on so he could see what he was doing. I didn't want to look.

The Mini had been so nice to drive. Such a good little car, and now it was smashed up, and I'd done it. I felt as if I'd killed it.

Ted got back in the truck and said, "Hang on to your tea, I'll need to turn this round. Might bump a bit."

He turned the truck in a gateway and backed it up. Then he fixed a tow rope on the Mini. I'd seen him do that to other cars, but this was different.

We started out slowly along the lane, towing the Mini behind us.

"Just as well you didn't take a customer's car," he said. "Not easy to explain without getting you into big trouble."

I put my hand over my face and shook my head. He was right. A customer would have gone to the police. I'd have been done for under-age driving with no tax or insurance. Stealing, too, maybe. No driving licence. Big, big trouble.

"As it is," Ted went on, "I think the Mini will have to be your birthday present. If you mend it, you'll learn just about all there is to learn."

I took my hand off my face and looked at him. "You think it *can* be mended? You won't have to scrap it?"

"Can't tell until I look in the morning," Ted said. "If it's worth doing, it'll be a lot of work. But that's what I mean about a lot of learning."

Then he went on driving and didn't say any more.

****

Mum had hot soup ready.

She didn't say anything either, just hugged me.

Chapter 6
Now

That was in the summer. It's September now, and I've left school. I'm still working on the Mini.

The engine is OK. The steam I saw in the crash was from the smashed radiator.

The air filter had gone, and the brake hoses were leaking. Ted said we'd fit a new timing belt while we were at it. We had to re-build all the front of the car, and one of the wheels was bust. We fitted a new wing and a new bonnet, but there are still a lot of bashes and dents, and it will need a total re-spray. I'm putting masking tape on the windows.

Alan comes to help sometimes. I'm doing maths with him at the evening class. I thought it would be boring, but I understand it better now, and it's OK. Not boring. One day, maybe Alan and I will both be mechanics.

****

Mum and I talked about Dad.

"You loved him and so did I," she said. "I didn't want to say anything bad about him to you. But he was not a good driver, Deb. He was dangerous. He drove too fast. I worried every time he was out. I dreamed he would kill himself. When he hit that tree, it was like I'd been expecting it."

"I dreamed, too," I said. And we hugged for a long time.

****

Mick came in for petrol last week, but I got Ted to serve him.

Ted didn't mind. He said, "It's all money."

I suppose he's right.

Barrington Stoke would like to thank all its readers for commenting on the manuscript before publication and in particular:

Sam Armstrong

Kathy Arthur

Katie Bowes

Hidie Clay

Babli Digpal

Helen Pallett

Oliver Ritson

Sophie Springate

Become a Consultant!

Would you like to give us feedback on our titles before they are published? Contact us at the address below – we'd love to hear from you!

Email: info@barringtonstoke.co.uk
Website: www.barringtonstoke.co.uk

Also by the same author...

Smoke
by Alison Prince

For Dan it's just a dull train trip with his dad and his sister.

That's until Dad gets off for a smoke. And the train leaves without him.

How will they cope alone at night in the big city?

You can order *Smoke* directly from our website at
www.barringtonstoke.co.uk

Also by the same author...

Luck
by Alison Prince

NO LUCK FOR DALE

Dale hates school.

He has no luck with girls.

He fights with his mum.

So how did he get to be a hero?

You can order *Luck* directly from our website at
www.barringtonstoke.co.uk

If you loved this book,
why don't you read ...

Stray

by David Belbin

**EVEN IN A GANG,
SHE'S ON HER OWN**

Stray's in with the wrong lot.

Can Kev save her?

Or will she drag him down?